Hoppelpopp
AND THE
Best Bunny

by MIRA LOBE

illustrated by
ANGELIKA
KAUFMANN

Holiday House / New York

Binny, Benny, Bernie, Bonnie, and Buddy
lived together in a warm, cozy burrow.
When they slept, they cuddled up
close to each other . . .

. . . so close that when Buddy had
bad dreams, the others could wake
up and shoo them away.

On rainy days the bunnies played
in their many underground tunnels.

When the sun was shining, the bunnies played outside. They played **Tail Tag** and **Tease**. They played **Look Out! The Fox Is Coming!** and **Hide-and-Seek in the Hazelnut Hedge**.

The rabbits shared everything. When Bonnie found a good hill for rolling, she told Benny, Bernie, Binny, and Buddy; and they all rolled together.

When Benny found a leaf pile to jump in, he told Binny, Bernie, Bonnie, and Buddy; and they all jumped together.

And when Binny found a carrot, Bernie a cabbage, and Buddy some clover, they told the others so everyone could share the feast.

One day a stranger came along—a great big rabbit named Hoppelpopp. They all rubbed noses because that's how rabbits greet each other.

"Which of you is the best bunny?" Hoppelpopp asked.
Binny, Benny, Bernie, Bonnie, and Buddy didn't
understand the question.

"The best," Hoppelpopp tried to explain, "is the fastest, the strongest, the smartest, the bravest . . . the best!"

"We're the same," said the bunnies. "We are all fast, strong, smart, and brave."

"That's not possible," said Hoppelpopp.
"We will have a competition. Run down
the hill, around the hedge, and back."
    And so they did.
    Binny was back first.
    "Binny is the fastest," said Hoppelpopp.
    "I am the fastest," Binny said proudly.
"I am better than the rest of you."

Benny was mad. "Don't show off," Benny said. He pushed Binny and knocked her down. Binny pushed back. Soon all five bunnies were hitting, scratching, and biting. Binnie, Bernie, Bonnie, and Buddy grew tired of fighting. But Benny didn't want to stop.

"Benny is the strongest," said Hoppelpopp.

Benny was proud. "I am the strongest. I am better than the rest of you."

"Let's see who's the smartest," said Hoppelpopp. "There's some lettuce on the other side of that fence. The first to get the lettuce is the smartest."

Binny ran around looking for a hole in the fence. Benny tried to bite the fence. And Bonnie and Buddy tried to climb it.

Meanwhile Bernie dug a hole, slipped under the fence, and brought back the lettuce.

"Bernie is the smartest," said Hoppelpopp, "and he gets to eat the lettuce."

So Bernie got to eat the lettuce all by himself. "I'm the smartest," he mumbled with his mouth full of leaves, "and I am better than the rest of you."

Then Hoppelpopp hopped to the creek
to find out who was the bravest. "Follow
me!" he said as he swam to the other side.
But none of the bunnies would follow.

Hoppelpopp tried to lure them with a
carrot. "Who will come and get it?" he called.

Bonnie dipped a forepaw into the water and pulled it out again. She dipped the other forepaw into the water and pulled it out again. Then she put both forepaws and both hind paws into the water and swam across the creek.

"Bonnie is the bravest," said Hoppelpopp. Bonnie proudly munched on her carrot.

"I am the bravest!" she called across the creek. "I am better than you are."

From that day on, everything changed.
The bunnies didn't eat together anymore. They
didn't sleep together anymore. And they didn't
play together anymore.

No one wanted to run because all the bunnies
already knew that Binny was the fastest.

No one wanted to wrestle because all the bunnies knew that Benny was the strongest.

Bernie didn't think any of the others was smart enough to talk to him.

And Bonnie had no respect for bunnies who were too scared to cross the creek.

Buddy cried because he wasn't best at anything. And because he wasn't fastest, strongest, smartest, or bravest, no one would wake him from his bad dreams.

Buddy suddenly cocked his ears. Someone was coming. He sniffed. The visitor didn't smell like a rabbit. It smelled like an enemy. Buddy drummed the ground with his hind legs. In rabbit language that means "Danger! Look out!"

The other bunnies rushed right over.

"A badger!" shouted Buddy. "There he is!"

The five ran away as fast as they could when Buddy had an idea. "Badgers are good at toddling," he said, "but rabbits are better at running. Let's turn around and chase him away."

And that's what they did.

"Buddy is the best," said Binny, Benny, Bernie, and Bonnie. "He is smart *and* brave."

"No," said Buddy. "I am only brave because the five of us are together."

Then Binny, Benny, Bernie, Bonnie, and Buddy—feeling equally proud and equally excited—ran back to their burrow . . .

. . . where they cuddled up close . . . so close that
when Buddy had bad dreams, the others could wake
up and shoo them away.

And Hoppelpopp hopped away. He
didn't find the best bunny, but he did
find five equally good ones.

Copyright © 2010 by G&G Verlag GmbH, Vienna

First published in Austria as DANN RUFEN ALLE HOPPELPOPP by G&G Verlag GmbH.

First published in the United States of America in 2015 by Holiday House, New York,

by arrangement with G&G Verlag GmbH.

English translation by Cäcilie Kovács

English translation copyright © 2015 by G&G Verlag GmbH

All Rights Reserved

HOLIDAY HOUSE is registered in the U.S. Patent and Trademark Office.

Printed and Bound in October 2014 at Tien Wah Press, Johor Bahru, Johor, Malaysia.

www.holidayhouse.com

First American Edition

1 3 5 7 9 10 8 6 4 2

Library of Congress Cataloging-in-Publication Data

Lobe, Mira.

[Dann Rufen Alle Hoppelpopp. English]

Hoppelpopp and the best bunny / by Mira Lobe ; illustrated by Angelika Kaufmann ; English translation by Cäcilie Kovács. — First American edition.

pages cm

"First published in Austria as DANN RUFEN ALLE HOPPELPOPP by G&G Verlag GmbH."

Summary: Bunnies Binny, Benny, Bernie, Bonnie, and Buddy love doing everything together until Hoppelpopp, a great big rabbit,

challenges them to a competition that will determine which of them is the best.

ISBN 978-0-8234-3287-5 (hardcover)

[1. Competition (Psychology)—Fiction. 2. Brothers and sisters—Fiction. 3. Rabbits—Fiction.]

I. Kaufmann, Angelika, illustrator. II. Kovács, Cäcilie, translator. III. Title.

PZ7.L7793Hop 2015

[E]—dc23

2014012319